Moving Day

by Fran Manushkin

illustrated by Tammie Lyon

raintree

a Capstone company — publishers for children

Raintree is an imprint of Capstone Global Library Limited, a company
incorporated in England and Wales having its registered office at 264 Banbury
Road, Oxford, OX2 7DY – Registered company number: 6695582

www.raintree.co.uk
myorders@raintree.co.uk

Text © Capstone Global Library Limited 2019
The moral rights of the proprietor have been asserted.

Art Director: Kay Fraser
Graphic Designer: Emily Harris
Production Specialist: Michelle Biedscheid
Printed and bound in India

ISBN 978 1 4747 8222 7
23 22 21 20 19
10 9 8 7 6 5 4 3 2 1

British Library Cataloguing in Publication Data
A full catalogue record for this book is available from
the British Library.

Acknowledgements
Fran Manushkin, pg. 26
Tammie Lyon, pg. 26

Contents

Chapter 1
Dear new girl

Katie's family was moving.

"You will love our new

house," said Katie's mum.

"I like this one!" said Katie.

"Why can't we stay here?"

"Your mum has a great new job," said Katie's dad. "We want to live close to it."

"Who will get my old bedroom?" Katie asked.

"Another girl like you," said Katie's mum.

"I will write her a note," Katie decided.

"Dear new person," she wrote. "I hope you like this room. I loved it so much! Sincerely, Katie Woo."

Chapter 2
A weird house

The Woo family drove away.

Katie's dad said, "Our new bathroom is great. It has a whirlpool bath."

"A whirlpool?" thought Katie. "What if I spin around and around and never stop?"

"Our new house has a sunken living room," said Katie's mum.

"Uh-oh," thought Katie, "what if I sink down into the floor and disappear? This house sounds weird!"

Suddenly, there it was!

The new house!

"It doesn't look spooky,"

thought Katie. "But you

never know."

Katie peeked into the
living room. "It's not sunken!"
she said.

"Not really!" Her dad
smiled. "It's called 'sunken'
because it's a few steps
down."

"Very fancy!" said Katie.

In the bathroom, Katie asked, "Where's the scary whirlpool?"

"It's not scary," said her mum. She turned on the whirlpool.

"Wow!" Katie said. "It's great for bubble baths!"

Suddenly, they heard a
loud wailing. It was coming
from the attic.

"Oh no!" Katie yelled.

"This house is haunted!"

Then a girl came running
into the house. She raced
upstairs.

Seconds later,
she came down,
holding a puppy.

"My puppy escaped from his travel box and hid in the attic. We almost left without him!" the girl said.

"I'm so glad you didn't," said Katie.

Chapter 3
Feels like home

Katie went to her bedroom

to unpack.

Outside her window, she

saw birds building a nest.

"You are my new neighbours,"

Katie said with a smile.

Soon, Katie smelled

something wonderful.

"Mum is making wonton

soup!" she said.

Katie heard

pretty music too.

"And Dad is

playing the piano." Katie

smiled. "This place is starting

to feel like home."

As the family ate their lunch, Katie wondered, "Where's my bed?"

"I don't know," said her mum. "The shop said it's coming today."

"I can sleep in the whirlpool bath," Katie teased. "It might be cosy, but my blanket will get very wet."

Just then, the doorbell rang, and in came Katie's bed.

"It's a bunk bed!" she yelled. "I can have sleepovers with Pedro and JoJo."

At bedtime, the moon shone into Katie's room. It lit up a piece of paper in the corner.

It was a note! Katie read it.

"Dear new girl, I hope you like this room. I did! A lot!"

"I love it!" Katie decided.

"Good night, new room!" she chanted, and she fell asleep.

About the author

Fran Manushkin is the author of many popular picture books, including *Baby, Come Out!*; *Latkes and Applesauce: A Hanukkah Story*; *The Belly Book* and *Big Girl Panties*. There is a real Katie Woo – she's Fran'sgreat-niece – but she never gets in half the trouble that Katie Woo does in the books. Fran writes on her beloved Mac computer in New York City, USA, without the help of her two naughty cats, Chaim and Goldy.

About the illustrator

Tammie Lyon began her love for drawing at a young age while sitting at the kitchen table with her dad. She continued her love of art and eventually attended college, where she earned a bachelors degree in fine art. After a brief career as a professional ballet dancer, she decided to devote herself full time to illustration. Today she lives with her husband, Lee, in Cincinnati, Ohio, USA. Her dogs, Gus and Dudley, keep her company as she works in her studio.

Glossary

disappear to go out of sight

fancy very special or decorated

sincerely in an honest and truthful way

sunken below other areas nearby

wailing letting out a long, loud cry of sadness
or pain

whirlpool a current of water that moves in a
circle and pulls floating objects towards its centre

Discussion questions

1. At first, Katie was unsure about moving. Why do you think she felt that way?

2. Katie's new house felt more like home after she smelled her mum's soup and heard her dad playing the piano. What sights, sounds or smells remind you of your home?

3. Do you think it would be fun to move house? Why or why not?

Writing prompts

1. Pretend you are moving. Write a letter to the person who will move into your room.

2. Katie's new house has some special things, like a whirlpool tub and a sunken living room. Write a sentence about something special in your home.

3. Make a list of ten words that describe your home.

Having fun
with Katie Woo

In *Moving Day*, Katie watches a bird build a nest outside her window. You can make your own nest with this fun project.

What you need:

- a brown paper bag
- craft glue
- dried leaves, grass and flowers
- optional: a bird and eggs from a craft shop

What you do:

1. Open up the paper bag. Pull the bottom of the bag up towards the top. As you do this, the sides will crumple. Work with your bag to make it into a bowl shape.

2. Apply some glue to the bag then stick a leaf on it. Repeat until your bag is covered with leaves. You can also glue on flowers or other lightweight items to decorate your bag.

3. Fill the bag with dried grass. If you would like, add a bird and eggs. Now you have a nest that looks as great as the real thing! Put it on a shelf or table for a pretty decoration.